The EASTER EGG

JAN BRETT

The
EASTER
EGG

SCHOLASTIC INC.
New York Toronto London Auckland
Sydney Mexico City New Delhi Hong Kong

Thank you rabbit models
"Squiggles" Carr, "Crystal" Coulihan, "Lefty" and "Righty" Megrath,
"Tikki" Fitts Mill, "Traffic" Nave, "Nibbles" Whiteman,
and Tom Roebuck's Buff Cochin chickens.

ISBN 978-0-545-36429-4

12 11 10 9 8 7 6 5 4 3 2 1   11 12 13 14 15 16/0

Printed in the U.S.A.   08

First Scholastic printing, March 2011

Design by Marikka Tamura
Text set in Adobe Jenson
The art was done in watercolors and gouache.
Airbrush backgrounds by Joseph Hearne

For Mia

Cheer-rup! Cheer-rup! Spring is here!
"Time to start on my first-ever Easter egg!" Hoppi said.
Each year, the bunny who decorated the winning egg got
to help the Easter Rabbit hide the eggs on Easter morning.

Hoppi had been dreaming about being that bunny all year long.

Now it was time to get started.

Everywhere Hoppi looked, rabbits were working on dazzling eggs.

I need an amazing idea, he thought.

Hoppi spotted Flora Bunny planting spring wildflowers in her eggs. *The Easter Rabbit will love those colorful flowers*, he thought, and started picking flowers for his egg.

"Here's a basket for your flowers, Hoppi," Flora said.

Chop, chop, scrape, scrape. Hoppi spied Buster Birch carving
a magnificent wooden egg.
"I wish I had some wood for my egg," he wished out loud.

"Here you go, Hoppi," Buster Birch said, and he put
a smooth, round piece of wood in Hoppi's basket.
"Thank you, Buster," Hoppi said.

Hoppi was hopping along when the smell of sweetness led him out
of the woods and straight to the chocolate egg that Aunt Sassyfrass
was decorating with creamy frosting squiggles and bows.

"Hello, Hoppi," she said, and she put some chocolate squares in his basket.

"Hippety-hop!" Hoppi exclaimed. "I'll make the Easter Rabbit a chocolate egg so sweet, it will make his whiskers tingle."

Then Hoppi saw Granny Ireney decorating one of her fabulous story eggs. First, she traced a design on the egg with a special tool. Then she dipped the egg in pots of yellow, green, orange and red dye, adding to the design each time.

Hoppi couldn't believe his eyes. "I'll never make an egg that beautiful," he told Granny Ireney.

She smiled. "Try," she said, giving him one of her special tools.

Hoppi was hopping by Hans Vanderabbit's garden when he
spotted an extraordinary egg. Hans was painting a portrait of
the Easter Rabbit so real that he looked alive.

"Fantastic!" Hoppi exclaimed.

"Thank you, Hoppi," Hans said. "Why don't you make a painting
on your egg?" He gave Hoppi pots of paint and a fine brush.

As Hoppi bounced along, a loud boing nearly knocked him off his feet. It was a whirling, twirling mechanical egg.

"Whoa!" Hoppi said. "That's an unusual egg."

"Would you like to make one?" Roberto asked.

Hoppi tried hard, but the harder he tried, the more parts and
pieces piled up around him.

"Thank you, Roberto," he sighed, "but I think I better make
the egg that is right for me."

Hoppi hopped back to the woods and lay down
under a tall tree to think.

Making a beautiful egg is harder than I imagined, he thought.
I guess I don't have to win. I just want to make an egg I am proud of.

Suddenly the woods rang with the squawking of birds sounding
an alarm. Mother Robin swooped down, calling wildly, as if she
couldn't decide where to go.

An egg had tumbled out of Mother Robin's nest. Inside the perfect
blue egg was a baby robin that needed its mother to keep it warm until
it hatched.

Hoppi knew what he had to do. He sat down carefully
and covered the blue egg with his soft, warm fur.

"I'll take care of you the best I can," he whispered. Relieved,
Mother Robin chirped and settled down on her other two eggs.

Hoppi never left the robin's egg. If it was sunny and warm, he carefully turned the egg in its nest of moss. If it was rainy and cold, he kept the egg covered and dry.

At night wild animals passed by. Hoppi crouched down and stayed
hidden in the ferns. Often he heard strange noises coming from above.
But Hoppi didn't run away.

Every day, the rabbits worked on their eggs. Tadpoles turned into
frogs, buds swelled into leaves and Easter came closer and closer.

Finally it was time for the rabbits to take their eggs to the glen.
They had forgotten all about Hoppi, who was quietly sitting on
the blue egg under the tall tree in the woods.

Early the next morning, the rabbits waited for the Easter Rabbit.
Suddenly a beautiful wagon rolled toward them out of the mist . . .

. . . and stopped. The Easter Bunny stepped down from
the wagon and admired the decorated eggs, one by one.

"You have brought me the most beautiful eggs in the world.

But a very special one is not here," he told them.

The rabbits were puzzled. Whose egg could it be?

"Fill my wagon with your wonderful eggs," he said.

"When I return, I will show it to you."

And he disappeared into the woods.

He came back with Hoppi, looking scruffy and bedraggled.

"Hoppi has an amazing egg to be proud of," the Easter Rabbit told them.

"He has kept Mother Robin's egg warm and safe until her baby bird hatched and she could take care of it."

The Easter Rabbit placed the empty blue shell in the place of honor
atop the wagon.

Now they were ready to go.

The rabbits cheered for the egg that had surprised them all.

"It's our best Easter ever, Hoppi!" they shouted.

Then the brave little bunny and the Easter Rabbit rode off together
to hide the eggs for girls and boys to find on Easter morning.